Library of Congress catalog card number: 2006920329
ISBN-10: 0-06-088274-3 — ISBN-13: 978-0-06-088274-7

Typography by Scott Richards
❖

Charlotte's Web™

The Perfect Word

Adapted by Catherine Hapka

Based on the Motion Picture Screenplay by Susanna Grant and

Karey Kirkpatrick

Based on the book by E. B. White

HarperEntertainment

An Imprint of HarperCollins*Publishers*

Templeton the rat lived by his own rules. And his number-one rule was: Every rat for himself.

But when Wilbur the pig came to the barn, things started to change.

First Wilbur made friends with Charlotte the spider. Before long he was friends with everyone—even Templeton.

But then something terrible happened. Templeton accidentally told Wilbur a secret: Come Christmastime, Wilbur would be turned into sausage and bacon'

Charlotte knew she had to save her friend from the terrible fate he'd been told. She just didn't know how. Then . . . she had an idea.

She did what she did best. She spun a beautiful web with the words "Some Pig" in it.

People came from all over town to see the web. That saved Wilbur . . . for a while. But soon Charlotte needed more words to spin.

That was where Templeton came in.

"That rat is always drag-drag-dragging in trash with writing on it," Gussy the goose pointed out.

At first Templeton refused to help. But then he realized something: having a pig around meant lots of scraps for him to eat.

So off he went to the dump to find more words to save Wilbur.

A pair of crows sat on a sign. They spotted Templeton scurrying toward the mounds of trash.

"Want to go mess with him?" one crow asked.

"Sounds like fun," the other replied.

The crows cawed and dive-bombed Templeton. He darted into a coffee can, just in time.

"The rat is not enjoying this!" Templeton muttered.
He was almost ready to give up.

Finally the crows flew away. Templeton spotted a newspaper.

"Hey, look," he said. "Words."

He ripped off a piece of the newspaper and carried it back to the barn.

Charlotte used the word "radiant" from the newspaper. And again, people came from all over to see her miraculous web.

But then Mr. Zuckerman decided to take Wilbur to the County Fair. If Wilbur didn't win a prize, he would be turned into dinner after all!

Charlotte couldn't let that happen. She needed another word.

Once again, Templeton refused to help. "What's in it for the rat?" he asked.

The geese told him exactly what was in it for him: food! At the fair there would be sticky, greasy, half-eaten, glorious food everywhere he looked!

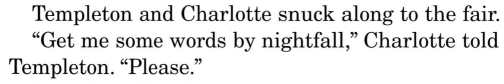

Templeton and Charlotte snuck along to the fair.

"Get me some words by nightfall," Charlotte told Templeton. "Please."

"You do realize I'm just here for the food, right?" Templeton grumbled.

But he went out and found more words for Charlotte.

Wilbur looked on as she worked all night to spin another web.

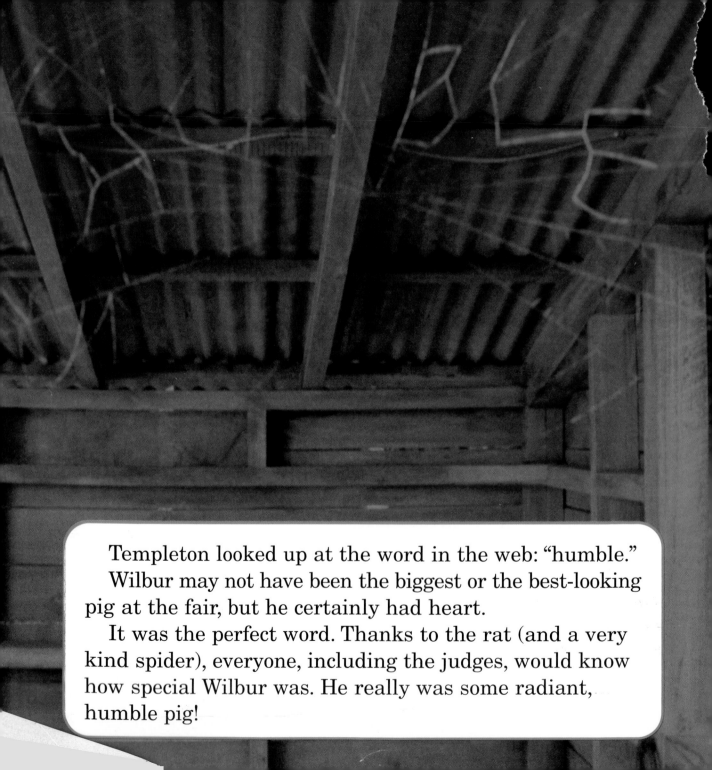

Templeton looked up at the word in the web: "humble."

Wilbur may not have been the biggest or the best-looking pig at the fair, but he certainly had heart.

It was the perfect word. Thanks to the rat (and a very kind spider), everyone, including the judges, would know how special Wilbur was. He really was some radiant, humble pig!